Thomas Wentworth Higginson

The Monarch of Dreams

Thomas Wentworth Higginson

The Monarch of Dreams

ISBN/EAN: 9783743408128

Manufactured in Europe, USA, Canada, Australia, Japa

Cover: Foto ©Andreas Hilbeck / pixelio.de

Manufactured and distributed by brebook publishing software
(www.brebook.com)

Thomas Wentworth Higginson

The Monarch of Dreams

THE

MONARCH OF DREAMS

.

BY

THOMAS WENTWORTH HIGGINSON

———

BOSTON

LEE AND SHEPARD, PUBLISHERS

1887 .

THE MONARCH OF DREAMS.

Φάσμα δόξει δόμων ἀνάσσειν.

ÆSCHYLUS: *Agamemnon*, 391.

THE MONARCH OF DREAMS.

HE who forsakes the railways and goes wandering through the hill-country of New England, must adopt one rule as invariable. When he comes to a fork in the road, and is assured that both ways lead to the desired point, he must simply ask which road is the best; and, on its being pointed out, must at once take the other. Nothing can be easier than the explanation of this method. The passers-by will always recommend the new road, which keeps to the valley and avoids the hills; but the old road, deserted by the general public, ascends the steeper grades, and has a monopoly of the wider views.

Turning to the old road, you soon feel that both houses and men are, in a manner, stranded. They see very little of the world, and are under no stimulus to keep themselves in repair. You are wholly beyond the dreary sway of French roofs ; and the caricatures of good Queen Anne's day are far from you. If any farmhouse on the hill-road was really built within the reign of that much-abused potentate, it is probably a solid, square mansion of brick, three stories high, blackened with time, and frowning rather gloomily from some hilltop, — as essentially a part of the past as an Irish round-tower or a Scotch border-fortress. A branching elm-tree or two may droop above it. It is partly screened from the road by a lilac-hedge, and by what seems an unnecessarily large wood-pile. A low stone wall surrounds the ample barns and sheds, made of unpainted wood, and now gray with age ; and near these is a neglected garden, where phlox and pinks and tiger-lilies are intersected with irregular hedges of tree-box. The house looks upon gorgeous sunsets and distant mountain ranges, and lakes surrounded by pine and chestnut woods. Against a lurid sky, or in a brooding fog, it is as impressive in the landscape as a feudal castle ; and like that, it is almost deserted : human life has slipped away from it into the manufacturing village, swarming with French Canadians, in the valley below.

It was to such a house that Francis Ayrault had finally taken up his abode, leaving behind him the old family homestead in a Rhode-Island seaside town. A series of

domestic cares and watchings had almost
broken him down : nothing debilitates a man
of strong nature like the too prolonged and
exclusive exercise of the habit of sympathy.
At last, when the very spot where he was
born had been chosen as a site for a new
railway-station, there seemed nothing more
to retain him. He needed utter rest and
change; and there was no one left on earth
whom he profoundly loved, except a little
sunbeam of a sister, the child of his father's
second marriage. This little five-year-old
girl, of whom he was sole guardian, had been
christened by the quaint name of Hart, after
an ancestor, Hart Ayrault, whose moss-cov-
ered tombstone the child had often explored
with her little fingers, to trace the vanishing
letters of her own name.

The two had arrived one morning from

the nearest railway station to take possession
of the old brick farmhouse. Ayrault had
spent the day in unpacking and in consulta-
tions with Cyrus Gerry, — the farmer from
whom he had bought the place, and who was
still to conduct all out-door operations. The
child, for her part, had compelled her old
nurse to follow her through every corner of
the buildings. They were at last seated at
an early supper, during which little Hart was
too much absorbed in the novelty of wild red
raspberries to notice, even in the most casual
way, her brother's worn and exhausted look.

"Brother Frank," she incidentally re-
marked, as she began upon her second sau·
cerful of berries, "I love you!"

"Thank you, darling," was his mechanical
reply to the customary ebullition. She was
silent for a time, absorbed in her pleasing

pursuit, and then continued more specifically, " Brother Frank, you are the kindest person in the whole world! I am so glad we came here! May we stay here all winter? It must be lovely in the winter; and in the barn there is a little sled with only one runner gone. Brother Frank, I love you so much, I don't know what I shall do! I love you a thousand pounds, and fifteen, and eleven and a half, and more than tongue can tell besides! And there are three gray kittens, — only one of them is almost all white, — and Susan says I may bring them for you to see in the morning."

Half an hour later, the brilliant eyes were closed in slumber; the vigorous limbs lay in perfect repose; and the child slept that night in the little room inside her brother's, on the same bed that she had occupied ever since she had been left motherless. But her brother lay awake, absorbed in a project too fantastic to be talked about, yet which had really done more than any thing else to bring him to that lonely house.

There has belonged to Rhode-Islanders, ever since the days of Roger Williams, a certain taste for the ideal side of existence. It is the only State in the American Union where chief justices habitually write poetry, and prosperous manufacturers print essays on the Freedom of the Will. Perhaps, moreover, Francis Ayrault held something of these tendencies from a Huguenot ancestry, crossed with a strain of Quaker blood. At any rate it was there, and asserted itself at this crisis of his life. Being in a manner detached from almost all ties, he resolved to use his opportunity in a direction yet almost unexplored by man. His earthly joys being prostrate, he had resolved to make a mighty effort at self-concentration, and to render himself what no human being had ever yet been,—the ruler of his own dreams.

Coming from a race of day-dreamers, Ayrault had inherited an unusual faculty of dreaming also by night; and, like all persons having an especial gift, he perhaps over-estimated its importance. He easily convinced himself that no exertion of the intellect during wakeful hours, can for an instant be compared with that we employ in dreams. The finest brain-structures of Shakspeare or Dante, he reasoned, are yet but such stuff as dreams are made of; and the stupidest rustic, the most untrained mind, will sometimes have, could they be but written out, visions that surpass those of these masters. From the dog that hunts in dreams, up to Coleridge dreaming "Kubla Khan" and interrupted by the man on business from Porlock, every sentient, or even half-sentient, being reaches its height of imaginative action in dreams. In these alone, Ayrault reasoned, do we grasp something beyond ourselves : every other function is self-limited, but who can set a limit to his visions ? Of all forms of the Inner Light, they afford the very inmost ; in these is fulfilled the early maxim of Friends, —that a man never rises so high as when he knows not where he is going. On awaking, indeed, we cannot even tell where we have just been. Probably the very utmost wealth of our remembered dreams is but a shred and fragment of those whose memory we cannot grasp.

But Ayrault had been vexed, like all

others, by the utter incongruity of successive dreams. This sublime navigation still
waited, like that of balloon voyages, for a rud-
der. Dreams, he reasoned, plainly try to con-
nect themselves. We all have the frequent
experience of half-recognizing new situations
or even whole trains of ideas. We have seen
this view before; reached this point; struck
in some way the exquisite chord of memory.
When half-aroused, or sometimes even long
after clear consciousness, we seem to draw a
half-drowned image of association from the
deep waters of the mind; then another, then
another, until dreaming seems inseparably
entangled with waking. Again, over nightly
dreams we have at least a certain amount of
negative control, sufficient to bring them to
an end. Ayrault had long since discovered
and proved to himself the fact, insisted upon

by Currie and Macnish, that a nightmare can be banished by compelling one's self to remember that it is unreal. Again and again, during sleep, had he cast himself from towers, dropped from balloons, fallen into the sea, — and all unscathed. This way of ending an unpleasant dream was but a negative power indeed; but it was a substantial one: it implied the existence of some completer authority. If we can stop motion, we can surely originate it. He had already searched the books, therefore, for recorded instances of more positive control.

There was opium of course; but he was one of those on whom opium has little exciting influence, and so far as it had any, it only made his visions more incoherent. Haschish was in this respect still worse. It was not to be thought of, that one should resort, for the sake of dreams, to raw meat, like Dryden and Fuseli; or to other indigestible food, like Mrs. Radcliffe. The experiments of Giron de Buzareingues promised a little more; for he actually obtained recurrent dreams. He used to sleep with his knees uncovered on cool nights, and fancied during his sleep that he was riding in a stage-coach, where the lower extremities are apt to grow cold. Again, by wearing a nightcap over the front part of his head only, he seemed, when asleep, to be uncovering before a religious procession, and feeling chilly in the nape of the neck; this same result being obtained on several different occasions. It was recorded of some one else, that, by letting his feet hang over the bedside, he repeatedly imagined himself tottering on the brink of a precipice. Even these crude and superficial

experiments had a value, Ayrault thought.
If coarse physical processes could affect the
mind's action, could not the will by some
more powerful levers control the silent rev-
eries of the night?

He derived some encouragement, too,
from such instances as that recorded of
Alderman Clay of Newark, England, during
the siege of that town by Cromwell. He
dreamed on three successive nights that his
house had taken fire. Because of this sup-
posed warning, he removed his family from
the dwelling ; and, when it was afterwards
really burned by Cromwell's troops, left a
bequest of a hundred pounds to supply
penny loaves to the town poor, in acknowl-
ment of his marvellous escape. It is true
that the three dreams were apparently mere
repetitions of one another, and in no way

continuous; it is true that they were not the result of any conscious will. So much the better: they were produced by the continuous working of some powerful mental influence; and this again was the result of external conditions. The experiment could not be reproduced. One could not be always dreaming under pressure of a cannonade by Cromwell, any more than Charles Lamb's Chinese people could be always burning down their houses in order to taste the flavor of roast-pig. But the point was, that if dreams could be made to recur by accidental circumstances, the same thing might perhaps be effected by conscious thought.

Now that he was in a position for free experiment, he hoped to accomplish something more substantial than any casual or vague results; and he therefore so arranged his methods as to avoid interruption. Instead of exciting himself by day, he adopted a course of strict moderation; took his food regularly with the little girl, amused by her prattle; began systematic exercise on horseback and on foot; avoided society and the newspapers; and went to bed at an early hour, locking himself into a wing of the large farmhouse, the little Hart sleeping in a room within his. Once retired, he did not permit himself to be called on any pretext. Hart always slept profoundly; and with her first call of waking in the morning, he rang the bell for old Susan, who took the child away. It would have left him more free, of course, to intrust her altogether to the nurse's charge, but to this he could not bring himself. She was his one sacred trust, and not even his beloved projects could wholly displace her.

The thought had occurred to him, long since, at what, point to apply his efforts for the control of his dreams. He had been quite fascinated, some time before, by a large photograph in a shop window, of the well-known fortress known as Mont Saint Michel, in Normandy. Its steepness, its airy height, its winding and returning stairways, its overhanging towers and machicolations, had struck him as appealing powerfully to that sense of the vertical, which is, for some reason or other, so peculiarly strong in dreams. We are rarely haunted by visions of plains; often of mountains. The sensation of uplifting or downlooking is one of our commonest nightly experiences. It seemed to Ayrault that by going to sleep with the vivid mental image in his brain of a sharp and superb altitude like that of Mont Saint Michel, he could avail himself of this magic, whatever it was, that lay in the vertical line. Casting himself off into the vast sphere of dreams, with the thread of his fancy attached to this fine image, he might risk what would next come to him ; as a spider anchors his web and then floats away on it. In the silence of the first night at the farmhouse, — a stillness broken only by the answering cadence of two whippoorwills in the neighboring pine-wood, — Ayrault pondered long over the beautiful details of the photograph, and then went to sleep.

That night he was held, with the greatest vividness and mastery, in the grasp of a dream such as he had never before expe-

rienced. He found himself on the side of
a green hill, so precipitous that he could
only keep his position by lying at full
length, clinging to the short soft grass, and
imbedding his feet in the turf. There were
clouds about him : he could see but a short
distance in any direction, nor was any sign
of a human being within sight. He was
absolutely alone upon the dizzy slope, where
he hardly dared to look up or down, and
where it took all his concentration of effort
to keep a position at all. Yet there was a
kind of friendliness in the warm earth; a
comfort and fragrance in the crushed herb-
age. The vision seemed to continue indefi-
nitely ; but at last he waked and it was
clear day. He rose with a bewildered feeling, and went to little Hart's room. The
child lay asleep, her round face tangled in

her brown curls, and one plump, tanned arm stretched over her eyes. She waked at his step, and broke out into her customary sweet asseveration, " Brother Frank, I love you ! "

Dismissing the child, he pondered on his first experiment. It had succeeded, surely, in so far as he had given something like a direction to his nightly thought. He could not doubt that it was the picture of Mont Saint Michel which had transported him to the steep hillside. That day he spent in the most restless anxiety to see if the dream would come again. Writing down all that he could remember of the previous night's vision, he studied again the photograph that had so touched his fancy, and then he closed his eyes. Again he found him-self — at some time between night and morning — on the high hillside, with the clouds around him. But this time the vapors lifted, and he could see that the hill stretched for an immeasurable distance on each side, always at the same steep slope. Everywhere it was covered with human beings, — men, women, and children, — all trying to pursue various semblances of occupation; but all clinging to the short grass. Sometimes, he thought — but this was not positive — that he saw one of them lose his hold and glide downwards. For this he cared strangely little; but he waked feverish, excited, trembling. At last his effort had succeeded: he had, by an effort of will, formed a connection between two dreams.

He came down to breakfast exhilarated and eager. What triumph of mind, what ranges of imagination equalled those now opening before him! As an outlet for his delight, he gave up the day to little Hart, always ready to monopolize. With her he visited the cows in the barn, the heifers in the pasture; heard their names, their traits, and — with much vagueness of arithmetic — their ages. She explained to him that Brindle was cross, and Mabel roguish; and that she had put her arm around little Pet's neck. Animals are to children something almost as near as human beings, because they have those attributes of humanity which children chiefly prize, — instinct and affection. Then Hart had the horses to exhibit, the pigs, a few sheep, and a whole poultry-yard of chickens. She was already initiated into the art and mystery of looking for hen's eggs, and indeed already trotted about after Cyrus Gerry, a little acolyte at the altar of farming. "She likes to play at it," said Cyrus, "same as my boys do: but just call it work, and — there ! I don't blame 'em. The fact is," he added apologetically, "neither me nor my boys like to be kept always at the same dull roundelay o'choppin' wood and doin' chores."

It was quite true that Cyrus Gerry and his boys, like many a New-England farm household, had certain tastes and aptitudes that sadly interfered with their out-door work. One son played the organ in the neighboring city, another was teaching himself the violin, and the third filled the barn with half-finished models of machinery. Cyrus himself read over and over again, in the winter evenings, his one favorite book, — a translation of Lamartine's "History of the Girondists," — pronounced habitually Guyrondists; and he found in its pages a pithy illustration for every event that could befall his chosen hero, Humanity. Most of his warnings were taken from the career of Robespierre, and his high and heroic examples from Vergniaud ; while these characters lost nothing in vigor by being habitually quoted as " Robyspierry," and " Virginnyord."

In the service of his little sister, Ayrault explored that day many an old barn and shed ; while she took thrilling leaps from the hay-mow or sat with the three gray kittens in her lap. Together they decked the parlors with gay masses of mountain laurel, or with the first-found red lilies, or with white water-lilies from the pond. To the child, life was full of incident on that lonely farm. One day it was a young woodchuck caught in a trap, and destined to be petted ; another day, the fearful assassination of a whole brood of young chickens by a culprit owl; the next, a startling downfall of a whole nest of swallows in the chimney. On this particular day she chattered steadily, and Ayrault enjoyed it. But that night he lost utterly the new-found control of his dream, and waked in irritation with himself and the world.

He spent the next day alone. It cost Hart a few tears to lose her new-found playmate, but a tame pigeon consoled her. That night Ayrault pondered long over his memoranda of previous dreaming, and over the photograph with which he had begun the spell, and was rewarded by a renewal of his visions; but this time wavering and uncertain. Sometimes he was again on the bare hillside, clutching at the soft grass; then the scene shifted to some castle, whose high battlements he was climbing ; then he found himself among the Alps, treading some narrow path between rock and glacier, with the tinkling herd of young goats crowding round him for comradeship and impeding his progress ; again, he was following the steep course of some dried brook among the Scottish Highlands, or pausing to count the deserted hearthstones of a vanished people. Always at short intervals he reverted to the grassy hill ; it seemed the foundation of his visions, the rest were like dreams within dreams. At last a heavier sleep came on, featureless and purposeless, till he waked unrefreshed.

On the following night he grasped his dream once more. Again he found himself on the precipitous slope, this time looking off through clear air upon that line of detached mountain peaks, Wachusett, Monadnock, Moosilauke, which make the southern outposts of New-England hills. In the valley lay pellucid lakes, set in summer beauty, — while he clung to his perilous hold. Presently there came a change; the mountain sank away softly beneath him, and the grassy slope remained a plain. The men and women, his former companions, had risen from their reclining postures and were variously busy; some of them even looked at him, but there was nothing said. Great spaces of time appeared to pass: suns rose and set. Sometimes one of the crowd would throw down his implements of labor, turn his face to the westward, walk swiftly away, and disappear. Yet some one else would take his place, so that the throng never perceptibly diminished. Ayrault began to feel rather unimportant in all this gathering, and the sensation was not agreeable.

On the succeeding night the hillside vanished, never to recur; but the vast plain remained, and the people. Over the wide landscape the sunbeams shed passing smiles of light, now here, now there. Where these shone for a moment, faces looked joyous, and Ayrault found, with surprise, that he could control the distribution of light and shade. This pleased him; it lifted him into conscious importance. There was, however, a singular want of all human relation in the tie between himself and all these people. He felt as if he had called them into being, which indeed he had; and could annihilate them at pleasure, which perhaps could not be so easily done. Meanwhile, there was a certain hardness in his state of mind toward them; indeed, why should a dreamer feel patience or charity or mercy toward those who exist but in his mind? Ayrault at any rate felt none; the sole thing which disturbed him was that they sometimes grew a little dim, as if they might vanish and leave him unaccompanied. When this happened, he drew with conscious volition a gleam of light over them, and thereby refreshed their life. They enhanced his weight in the universe: he would no more have parted with them than a Highland chief with his clansmen.

For several nights after this he did not dream. Little Hart became ill and his mind was pre-occupied. He had to send for physicians, to give medicine, to be up with the child at night. The interruption vexed him; and he was also pained to find that there seemed to be a slight barrier between himself and her. Yet he was rigorously faithful to his duties as nurse; he even liked to hold her hand, to sooth her pain, to watch her sweet, patient face. Like Coleridge in misanthropic mood, he saw, not felt, how beautiful she was. Then, with the rapidity of childish convalescence, she grew well again; and he found with joy that he could resume the thread of his dream-life.

Again he was on his boundless plain, with his circle of silent allies around him. Suddenly they all vanished, and there rose before him, as if built out of the atmosphere, a vast building, which he entered. It included all structures in one, — legislative halls where men were assembled by hundreds, waiting for him; libraries, where all the books belonged to him, and whole alcoves were filled with his own publications; galleries of art, where

he had painted many of the pictures, and
selected the rest. Doors and corridors led
to private apartments; lines of obsequious
servants stood for him to pass. There
seemed no other proprietor, no guests; all
was for him; all flattered his individual great-
ness. Suddenly it occurred to him that he
was painfully alone. Then he began to pass
eagerly from hall to hall, seeking an equal
companion, but in vain. Wherever he went,
there was a trace of some one just vanished,
— a book laid down, a curtain still waving.
Once he fairly came, he thought, upon the
object of his pursuit; all retreat was cut off,
and he found himself face to face with a
mirror that reflected back to him only his
own features. They had never looked to him
less attractive.

Ayrault's control of his visions became

plainly more complete with practice, at least as to their early stages. He could lie down to sleep with almost a perfect certainty that he should begin where he left off. Beyond this, alas! he was powerless. Night after night he was in the same palace, but always differently occupied, and always pursuing, with unabated energy, some new vocation. Sometimes the books were at his command, and he grappled with whole alcoves; sometimes he ruled a listening senate in the halls of legislation ; but the peculiarity was, that there were always menials and subordinates about him, never an equal. One night, in looking over these obsequious crowds, he made a startling discovery. They either had originally, or were acquiring, a strange resemblance to one another, and to some person whom he had somewhere seen.

All the next day, in his waking hours, this thought haunted him. The next night it flashed upon him that the person whom they all so closely resembled, with a likeness that now amounted to absolute identity, was himself.

From the moment of this discovery, these figures multiplied; they assumed a mocking, taunting, defiant aspect. The thought was almost more than he could bear, that there was around him a whole world of innumerable and uncontrollable beings, every one of whom was Francis Ayrault. As if this were not sufficient, they all began visibly to duplicate themselves before his eyes. The confusion was terrific. Figures divided themselves into twins, laughing at each other, jeering, running races, measuring heights, actually playing leap-frog with one another. Worst of all, each one of these had as much apparent claim to his personality as he himself possessed. He could no more retain his individual hold upon his consciousness than the infusorial animalcule in a drop of water can know to which of its subdivided parts the original individuality attaches. It became insufferable, and by a mighty effort he waked.

The next day, after breakfast, old Susan sought an interview with Ayrault, and taxed him roundly with neglect of little Hart's condition. Since her former illness she never had been quite the same; she was growing pale and thin. As her brother no longer played with her, she only moped about with her kitten, and talked to herself. It touched Ayrault's heart. He took pains to be with the child that day, carried her for a long drive, and went to see her Guinea-hen's eggs. That night he kept her up later than usual, instead of hurrying her off as had become his wont; he really found himself shrinking from the dream-world he had with such effort created. The most timid and shy person can hardly hesitate more about venturing among a crowd of strangers than Francis Ayrault recoiled, that evening, from the thought of this mob of intrusive persons, every one of whom reflected his own image. Gladly would he have undone the past, and swept them all away forever. But the shrinking was all on one side: the moment he sank to sleep, they all crowded upon him, laughing, frolicking, claiming detestable intimacy. No one among strangers ever longed for a friendly face, as he, among these intolerable duplicates, longed for the sight of a stranger. It was worse yet when the images grew smaller and smaller, until they had shrunk to a pin's length. He found himself trying with all his strength of will to keep them at their ampler size, with only the effect that they presently became no larger than the heads of pins. Yet his own individuality was still so distributed among them that it could not be distinguished from them ; but he found himself merged in this crowd of little creatures an eighth of an inch long.

As the days went on, old Susan kept repeating her warnings about Hart, and finally proposed to take her into her own room. "She does not get sound sleep, sir ; she complains of her dreams." — "Of what dreams ?" said Ayrault. "Oh, about you, sir," was the reply, "she sees you very often, and a great many people who look just like you." Ayrault sank back in his chair terrified. Was it not enough that his own life was hopelessly haunted by a turbulent kingdom of his own creating? but must the malign influence extend also to this innocent child? He watched Hart the next morning at breakfast — she looked pale and had circles under her eyes, and glanced at him timidly; her eager endearments were all gone. A terrible temptation crossed Ayrault's mind for a moment, to employ this unspoiled nature in the perilous path of experiments on which he had entered. It vanished from him as soon as it had presented itself. He would tread his course alone, and send the child away, rather then risk any transmitted peril for her young life. It may be that her dreams had only an accidental resemblance to his ; at any rate she was sent away on a visit, and they were soon forgotten.

After the child had gone, a feeling of deep sadness fell on Ayrault. By night he was tangled in the meshes of a dream-life that had become a nightmare ; by day there was now nothing to arouse him. The child's insatiable affection, her ardent ebullitions, were absent. Cyrus Gerry's watchful and speculative mind grew suspicious and critical.

"I shouldn't wonder," he said to his wife, "if there was gettin' to be altogether too much dreamin'. There was Robyspierry, he was what you might call a dreamer. But that Virginnyord he was much nigher my idee of an American citizen."

"Got somethin' on his mind, think likely ?"

said the slow and placid Mrs. Gerry, who seldom had much upon hers.

"Dunno as I know," responded Cyrus. "But there, what if he has? As I look at it, humanity, a-ploddin' over this planet, meets with consid'able many left-handed things. And the best way I know of is to summons up courage and put right through 'em."

Cyrus's conceptions of humanity might, however, rise to such touches of Wandering-Jew comprehensiveness as this, and yet not reach Ayrault, who went his way lonelier than ever.

Having long since fallen out of the way of action, or at best grown satisfied to imagine enterprises and leave others to execute them, he now, more than ever, drifted on from day to day. There had been a strike at the neighboring manufacturing village, and there was to be a public meeting, at which he was besought, as a person not identified with either party, to be present, and throw his influence for peace. It touched him, and he meant to attend. He even thought of a few things, which, if said, might do good; then forgot the day of the meeting, and rode ten miles in another direction. Again, when at the little post-office one day, he was asked by the postmaster to translate several letters in the French language, addressed to that official, and coming from an unknown village in Canada. They proved to contain anxious inquiries as to the whereabouts of a handsome young French girl, whom Ayrault had occasionally met driving about in what seemed doubtful company. His sympathy was thoroughly aroused by the anxiety of the poor parents, from whom the letters came. He answered them himself, promising to interfere in behalf of the girl; delayed, day by day, to fulfill the promise; and, when he at last looked for her, she was not to be found. Yet, while his power of efficient action waned, his dream-power increased. His little people were busier about him than ever, though he controlled them less and less. He was Gulliver bound and fettered by Lilliputians.

But a more stirring appeal was on its way to him. The storm of the Civil War began to roll among the hills; regiments were recruited, camps were formed. The excitement reached the benumbed energies of Ayrault. Never, indeed, had he felt such a thrill. The old Huguenot pulse beat strongly within him. For days, and even nights, these

thoughts possessed his mind, and his dreams
utterly vanished. Then there was a lull in
the excitement ; recruiting stopped, and his
nightly habit of confusing visions set in
again with dreary monotony. Then there
was a fresh call for troops. An old friend
of Ayrault's came to a neighboring village,
and held a noon-day meeting in one of the
churches to recruit a company. Ayrault lis-
tened with absorbed interest to the rousing.
appeal, and, when recruits were called for,
was the first to rise. It turned out that the
matter could not be at once consummated,
as the proper papers were not there. Other
young men from the neighborhood followed
Ayrault's example, and it was arranged that
they should all go to the city for regular en-
listment the next day. All that afternoon
was spent in preparations, and in talking with

other eager volunteers, who seemed to look
to Ayrault as their head.   It was understood,
they told him, that he would probably be an
officer in the company.   He felt himself a
changed being; he was as if floating in air.
and ready to swim off to some new planet.
What had he now to do with that pale
dreamer who had nourished his absurd im-
aginings until he had barely escaped being
controlled by them?   When they crossed
his mind it was only to make him thank God
for his escape.   He flung wide the windows
of his chamber.   He hated the very sight of
the scene where his proud vision had been
fulfilled, and he had been Monarch of Dreams.
No matter: he was now free, and the spell
was broken.   Life, action, duty, honor, a re-
deemed nation, lay before him; all entangle-
ments were cut away.

That evening there went a summons through the little village that opened the door of every house. A young man galloped out from the city, waking the echoes of the hills with his somewhat untutored bugle-notes, as he dashed along. Riding from house to house of those who had pledged themselves, he told the news. There had been a great defeat; reinforcements had been summoned instantly; and the half-organized regiment, undrilled, unarmed, not even uniformed, was ordered to proceed that night to the front, and replace in the forts round Washington other levies that were a shade less raw. Every man desiring to enlist must come instantly; yet, as before daybreak the regiment would pass by special train on the railway that led through the village, those in that vicinity might join it at the station, and

have still a few hours at home. They were
hurried hours for Ayrault, and toward mid-
night he threw himself on his bed for a
moment's repose, having left strict orders for
his awakening. He gave not one thought to
his world of visions; had he done so, it
would have only been to rejoice that he had
eluded them forever.

Let a man at any moment attempt his
best, and his life will still be at least half
made up of the accumulated results of past
action. Never had Ayrault seemed so absolutely safe from the gathered crowd of his
own delusions: never had they come upon
him with a power so terrific. Again he was
in those stately halls which his imagination
had so laboriously built up: again the mob
of unreal beings came around him, each more
himself than he was. Ayrault was beset,

encircled, overwhelmed ; he was in a manner lost in the crowd of himself. If any confused thought of his projected army-life entered his dream, it utterly subordinated itself ; or merely helped to emphasize the vastness and strengthen the sway of that phantom army to which he had given himself, and of which he was already the pledged recruit.

In the midst of this tumultuous dreaming, came confused sounds from without. There was the rolling of railway wheels, the scream of locomotive engines, the beating of drums, the cheers of men, the report and glare of fireworks. Mingled with all, there came the repeated sound of knocking at his own door, which he had locked, from mere force of habit, ere he lay down. The sounds seemed only to rouse into new tumult the figures of his dream. These suddenly began to in-

crease steadily in size, even as they had before diminished; and the waxing was more
fearful than the waning. From being Gulliver among the Lilliputians, Ayrault was
Gulliver in Brobdingnag. Each image of
himself, before diminutive, became colossal:
they blocked his path; he actually could not
find himself, could not tell which was he that
should arouse himself, in their vast and end-
less self-multiplication. He became vaguely
conscious, amidst the bewilderment, that the
shouts in the village were subsiding, the
illuminations growing dark; and the train
with its young soldiers was again in motion,
throbbing and resounding among the hills,
and bearing the lost opportunity of his life
away — away — away.

www.ingramcontent.com/pod-product-compliance
Lightning Source LLC
Chambersburg PA
CBHW022202020726
47496CB00008B/2840